Hop In!

Hop In!

Written by Julie Small-Gamby
Illustrated by David Slonim

SCHOLASTIC INC.

New York   Toronto   London   Auckland   Sydney
Mexico City   New Delhi   Hong Kong   Buenos Aires

Hop in, Cat.

Hop in, Rat.

3

Hop in, Pig.

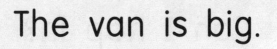

The van is big.

Can I hop in?

I am too big.

Hop out!

ISBN-13: 978-0-545-04570-4
ISBN-10: 0-545-04570-3

Text copyright © 2002 by Scholastic Inc.
Illustrations copyright © 2002 by David Slonim.
All rights reserved. Published by Scholastic Inc.
SCHOLASTIC, SCHOLASTIC READINGLINE,
and associated logos are trademarks and/or
registered trademarks of Scholastic Inc.

12 11 10 9 8 7 6 5 4 3 2 1   7 8 9 10 11 12/0

Printed in the U.S.A.   23

This edition first printing, October 2007